Usborne

The First
Christmas

Edited by Jane Chisholm

Additional design by Katrina Fearn

Digital manipulation by Mike Olley

Usborne

The First Christmas

Illustrated by

Elena Temporin

Retold by Heather Amery

Designed by Laura Fearn

Contents

Mary and the Angel

Mary lived a very long time ago in a little town called Nazareth. It was in an area called Galilee in Israel. When Mary grew up, her mother and father arranged for her to marry Joseph. He was a carpenter who lived in Nazareth. The day of the wedding had been set. Mary was happy. She looked forward to marrying Joseph. She knew he was a good, kind man.

6

One day, Mary was
alone, busy with the
work she did to help her
mother. Suddenly, she saw a
stranger in front of her. She was startled
and a little scared.

"Don't be afraid, Mary," said the stranger. "I am Gabriel,
an angel sent to you by God. He knows you and loves
you. God has sent me to tell you that He has chosen you
to be the mother of His Son. He will be the Son of God,
and His name will be Jesus. He will be a great King and
his kingdom will last forever."

Mary stared at Gabriel. She was still a little scared and very puzzled.

"I don't understand," she said. "How can I have a baby when I'm not married yet?"

"God can do anything. Nothing is too hard for Him," replied Gabriel. "You know your cousin Elizabeth was married for many years and never had any children. This made her very sad and she often prayed to God to have a child. God heard her prayers. Now she is old, but she is expecting a baby in a few months' time."

Mary thought for a while. She didn't really understand what Gabriel meant, but she loved and trusted God. She bowed her head and said, "I will do what God wants me to do."

When she looked up, Gabriel had gone and she was alone again.

Joseph's Dream

When Joseph heard that Mary was
expecting a baby, he was very worried.
He didn't know what to do.

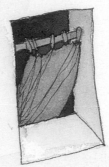

Joseph knew he wasn't the father of the baby.
Should he put off his marriage to Mary, he wondered?
Should he send her away where she could have her
baby very quietly, where no one in Nazareth would
know? Where no one could say bad things about her?
He thought and thought, wanting to do what was best
for Mary.

Then, one night,
Joseph had a
dream. In it an
angel sent by God
said to him, "Joseph,
don't be afraid to marry Mary. She has done nothing
wrong. Her son will be the Son of God. You will call him
Jesus. He will be a King and save his people."

When Joseph woke up the next morning, he thought
about his dream. He was amazed by what the angel had
told him, but he knew now what he had to do. He
quickly made new plans for his wedding to Mary and
soon they were married. They lived happily in his house,
and Joseph promised himself that he would always
take care of Mary and her baby son.

Journey to Bethlehem

Not long after Mary and Joseph were married, Emperor Augustus, who was the Roman ruler of Israel, made an order. All the people had to go to the town their families came from. There they had to register, so that the Emperor could make sure they paid their taxes.

Joseph's family was descended from King David. This meant that Joseph had to go to Bethlehem, where King David was born hundreds of years ago.

The journey to Bethlehem was a very long one and it would take many days. Mary was expecting her baby quite soon now, and Joseph didn't want to leave her at home. Together they packed up all the things they needed for the journey.

They loaded Joseph's donkey with warm clothes, food and water, and clothes for the baby. The road was dusty and stony, and they would have to stop for the night anywhere they could find a resting place.

When everything was ready, they shut up their house, and said goodbye to their families and friends. Then they began the long trek.

Joseph had to walk all the way. Mary walked too, but she rode on the donkey when she was tired. Joseph had to carry some of the baggage to make room for her on the donkey. He never complained. All the way, he talked to Mary, to keep her smiling and to stop her from worrying about her baby.

No Room at the Inns

At last Mary and Joseph reached the little town of Bethlehem. It was very late at night. The narrow streets were crowded with other people who had come to register for their taxes.

Joseph led the donkey along the streets, looking for somewhere he and Mary could sleep for the night. Mary was very tired. She knew her baby would be born very soon. Joseph knocked on the doors of all the inns they came to, asking for a room. Everywhere was already full. No one had any rooms left.

When they came to the very last inn, Joseph knocked on the door. He hoped that this inn would have a little space for them. The innkeeper opened the door.

17

18

Joseph asked if there was somewhere they could sleep for the night. The innkeeper said he couldn't take anyone in. He was already full to the roof.

He was just about to close the door when he looked at Mary. He could see how tired she was, and felt sorry for her. Holding out a small lamp, he said, "There's a stable over there. It's clean and empty. There's lots of clean straw and soft hay you could sleep on."

Joseph took the lamp and thanked the innkeeper for his kindness.

Then he led the donkey to the stable. He pushed open the door, and helped Mary down from the donkey.

Holding up the lamp, Joseph could see that the stable was just as the innkeeper had said. It was warm and clean, and would do very well for the night.

Born in a Stable

Joseph made a bed of straw for Mary on the floor of the stable, and laid his cloak over it. Then he and Mary ate some of the food they had brought with them. When they had finished, Mary lay down on the bed, very thankful that she could rest at last.

During the night, Mary gave birth to her baby. Joseph helped her to wash him and wrap him in warm clothes. Then he filled a manger with soft hay, and spread some clothes on it to make a bed.

Mary gently laid her little son in it, watching and singing to him until he went to sleep. "Jesus," she whispered, "your name is Jesus and you are the Son of God."

Shepherds on the Hills

On the hills outside Bethlehem a group of shepherds lay half-asleep around their camp fire. They were guarding their sheep. They knew there were some wild animals on the hills, which would try to snatch a sheep or a lamb during the night.

Suddenly, the shepherds saw a brilliant light shining in the dark sky. It was so bright, it lit up all the ground around them. Dazzled, they sat up, shielding their eyes and wondering what it could be. Then an angel appeared in front of them. They were very scared.

"Don't be frightened," said the angel. "I have wonderful news for you, and for all people. Tonight the Saviour, the Son of God, was born in a stable in Bethlehem. You will find the baby asleep in a manger."

As the shepherds stared in amazement at the angel, more angels appeared. Soon there was a huge crowd of them, all singing praises to God. "Glory to God in the highest, and peace to all people who love Him," they sang.

Then the light slowly faded and the angels were gone. For a while the shepherds were too surprised to speak. Slowly they got to their feet and began to talk about what they had seen and heard. They were very excited.

"We must go at once to Bethlehem," said one. "We must see this child," said another. "How will we know which is the right stable?" asked a third. "The angel said we would find him," replied another shepherd. "Don't waste any more time. We must hurry."

"What about the sheep?" asked one. "The angel wouldn't have told us to leave if they were in danger. Let's just take the lambs with us." replied another.

Together they started to run to the little town. Stumbling across the dark hills, they soon came to Bethlehem. Walking through the streets, they looked for a stable. At the end of the town, they saw a stable across a yard from an inn. It had a dim light shining from the door.

"That must be it," shouted a shepherd in excitement. "Don't make so much noise," whispered another. "You'll wake the baby. The angel said he'd be asleep."

In the stable, Mary heard the shepherds talking outside the door. Then the door slowly opened and a shepherd peered in. Mary smiled. He looked at her and then at the baby in the manger. Then he grinned with delight.

The shepherd turned his head and whispered to the others, "This is the right stable and there's the baby."

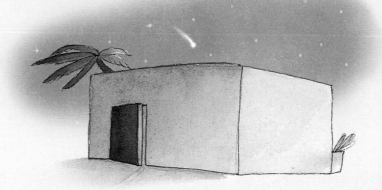

Together the shepherds crept into the stable as quietly as they could. They tiptoed up to the manger. Then they knelt down in the straw, gazing at the baby.

"We came because an angel told us that this baby is the Saviour, and the Son of God," said one of the shepherds to Mary and Joseph. Then he told them how they had been guarding their sheep on the hills, and how they had seen all the angels singing praises to God.

When it was time to go, the shepherds got quietly to their feet, and said goodbye to Mary and Joseph. With one last look at the baby, they walked out of the stable, closing the door behind them.

When they had gone, Mary gazed at her baby in the manger and thought about what the shepherds had told her. She wondered what it all meant.

Out in the streets of Bethlehem, the shepherds were so happy and excited, they sang songs of praise to God. They told everyone they met about the baby in the stable and what the angel had said to them. Then they hurried back to their sheep on the dark hills.

The Temple in Jerusalem

When Mary's son was eight days old, she and Joseph had a little ceremony and the baby was given his name of Jesus. Then Mary and Joseph got ready for a journey to take Jesus to Jerusalem.

When they reached the city, they went to the Temple. It was part of the Jewish law that the eldest son of every Jewish family should be promised to God in His Temple. So Mary and Joseph promised Jesus to God.

Living in the city was a very old man named Simeon. He was devoted to God, and had been told by God that he wouldn't die until he had seen the Saviour. He was waiting in the Temple when Mary and Joseph carried Jesus in. Smiling with joy, he walked up to them. Then he gently took the baby from Mary, and cradled him in his arms. Gazing at Jesus, Simeon said a prayer, and thanked God.

"God has kept his promise to me," said Simeon.

"Now I can die in peace. I have seen the Saviour, who will be a light for all people, and a glory for the people of Israel."

Mary and Joseph wondered what Simeon meant, but he didn't explain. He gave Mary her baby. Then he blessed them, and went happily on his way out of the Temple.

Also in the Temple was a widow named Anna. She was eighty-five years old, and spent all her days in the Temple, saying prayers to God. She saw Mary and Joseph, and looked at Jesus for a few silent moments. Then she said a prayer of thanks to God, and left the Temple. Hurrying through the streets of Jerusalem, she told everyone she met that the King they had been waiting for had come at last.

When Mary and Joseph had dedicated Jesus to God in the Temple, they took their baby son back again to Bethlehem where they stayed for many days.

Wise Men from the East

Far away, in a distant country in the East, some wise men saw a new, very bright star rising in the night sky. They were very excited. "Look, look at that," they cried. "What can it mean?" they asked each other. "It's a sign. It must mean something wonderful has happened," said one. "We must find out what it is," said another.

The wise men spent many days studying all the old books and records. After much discussion, one said, "I think this new star means that a King has been born." The others agreed. "We must go and find him," said one. "We'll go together," said another. "How will we know which way to go?" asked a third. "We'll follow the star. It will lead us," replied the first.

As soon as they were ready for a long journey, the wise men set off, taking presents for the new King. They rode at night, following the star that moved ahead of them, and resting during the heat of the day.

King Herod

When, at last, they reached Jerusalem, the wise men went to the palace of King Herod. They bowed low in front of the King, and one asked, "Where is the baby who is born to be King of the Jews? We saw his star rise in the East, and have followed it here. We want to find the King so that we can pay homage to him."

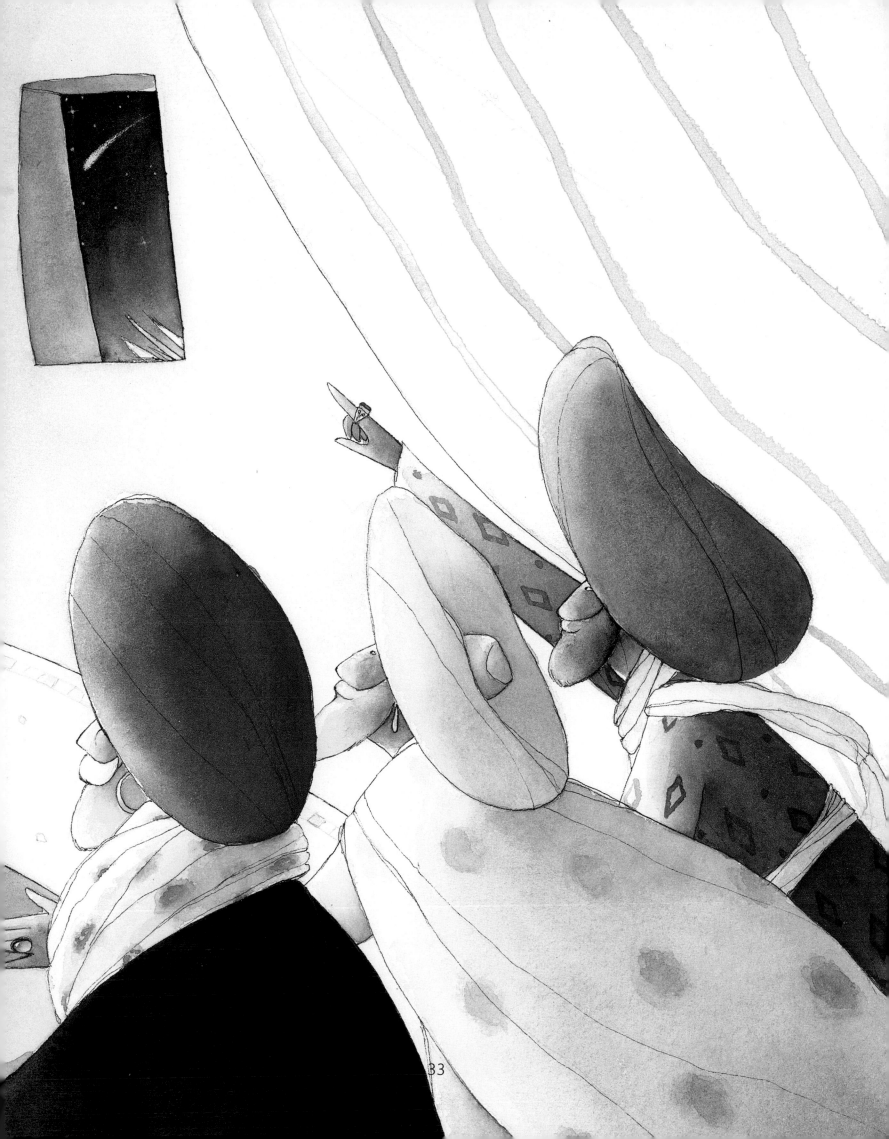

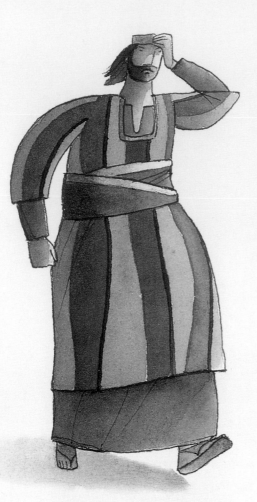

King Herod listened to the wise men, and was very worried. He couldn't answer their question. He hadn't heard of the new King. The Roman rulers of Israel had made him King of the Jews. "What will happen to me if there is another King?" he wondered.

The wise men left the palace, and asked the same question of the people they met in the streets of Jerusalem. Soon everyone was talking about the new King of the Jews.

King Herod summoned his chief priests and leaders of the people to the palace. He was angry and frightened. "I'm told that a King of the Jews has been born. Where is this King?" he demanded. The chief priests and leaders were afraid of King Herod. They talked together in whispers for a long time.

Then one said, "In Bethlehem, in Judaea." The others nodded in agreement. "A prophet wrote long ago that from Bethlehem would come a governor who would rule the people of Israel," added another.

King Herod ordered them to leave, and thought about what he should do. He sent a message to the wise men that they were to come secretly to the palace.
When they arrived, he commanded, "Go and search for the child in Bethlehem. When you have found him, come back and tell me. Then I, too, can go and pay homage to him."

Bethlehem

The wise men began the journey on to Bethlehem, the star still guiding them at night. Then it stopped over the house where Mary and Joseph were staying. The wise men sat looking at it for a moment, then quickly jumped down from their camels.

"We've come at last to the right place," cried one, laughing with excitement. "Let's go in and see the King," said another, smiling with great joy.

They knocked on the door, pushed it open, and went in. Inside, they knelt in front of Jesus, and explained to Mary why they had come. Then they gave her the presents they had brought with them; gold, sweet-smelling frankincense, and a special ointment called myrrh.

Mary gazed at the strange gifts for a baby, but smiled and thanked the wise men. Then they got to their feet, and left, closing the door quietly behind them.

"We must now go back to Jerusalem and tell King Herod what we have seen," said one of the wise men. They began their journey back to the city, camping for the first night outside Bethlehem.

In the morning, one said, "Last night I had a dream. In it an angel warned me that King Herod plans to kill the new King we have just seen." The others said that they'd had the same dream. "What shall we do?" asked one. "We must not go back to King Herod," replied another.

They quickly packed up, and loaded everything onto their camels. Then the wise men began their journey, not to Jerusalem, but home to their own country by a different route.

Joseph's Second Dream

A few nights later, Joseph also had a dream. In it an angel, sent by God, said to him, "Get up, and take the young child and Mary, his mother, to Egypt. Go as quickly as you can. King Herod wants to find the child and kill him. Stay in Egypt until I tell you it's safe for you to go home."

Joseph woke up at once. It was still dark. He woke Mary and together they hurriedly packed up their things, food and clothes, and loaded their donkey. Carrying Jesus, they journeyed through the night, terribly afraid King Herod's men would chase and catch them.

Mary and Joseph walked on, day after day, trudging along the stony, dusty roads, hardly daring to rest. At last, they came to Egypt. There they could stop, knowing they and Jesus were safe. King Herod's soldiers could not reach them there.

Death in Bethlehem

In Jerusalem, King Herod waited and waited for the wise men to return from Bethlehem. At last, he realized he had been tricked. They were not coming. He was furious. He gave an order that all boys under two years old in Bethlehem were to be killed.

His soldiers carried out his orders, finding and killing all the little boys. Throughout Bethlehem, mothers wept and mourned for their dead babies. The people of Israel had always hated their cruel rulers, but now they hated them even more.

Home at Last

Far away in Egypt, Mary, Joseph and Jesus lived in safety. Then King Herod died, and, one night, Joseph had another dream. In it, an angel sent by God said to him, "It is safe now for you to take Mary and Jesus home to Israel. The people who wanted to kill the young child are dead."

When Joseph woke up the next morning, he told Mary about his dream. Thankfully, they packed up their things again, and set off with Jesus on the long journey home. When Joseph heard that King Herod's son ruled in his place, he decided it would be safer for them to avoid Jerusalem and go back by way of Galilee. At last, they reached the small town of Nazareth, and were very happy to be able to settle down again in their own home.

Mary often thought about all the things that had happened when Jesus was born. She thought about the journeys they had made, Joseph's dreams, the shepherds and the wise men, and Simeon and Anna in the Temple in Jerusalem. And, most of all, she thought about her son, Jesus, who was the Son of God.

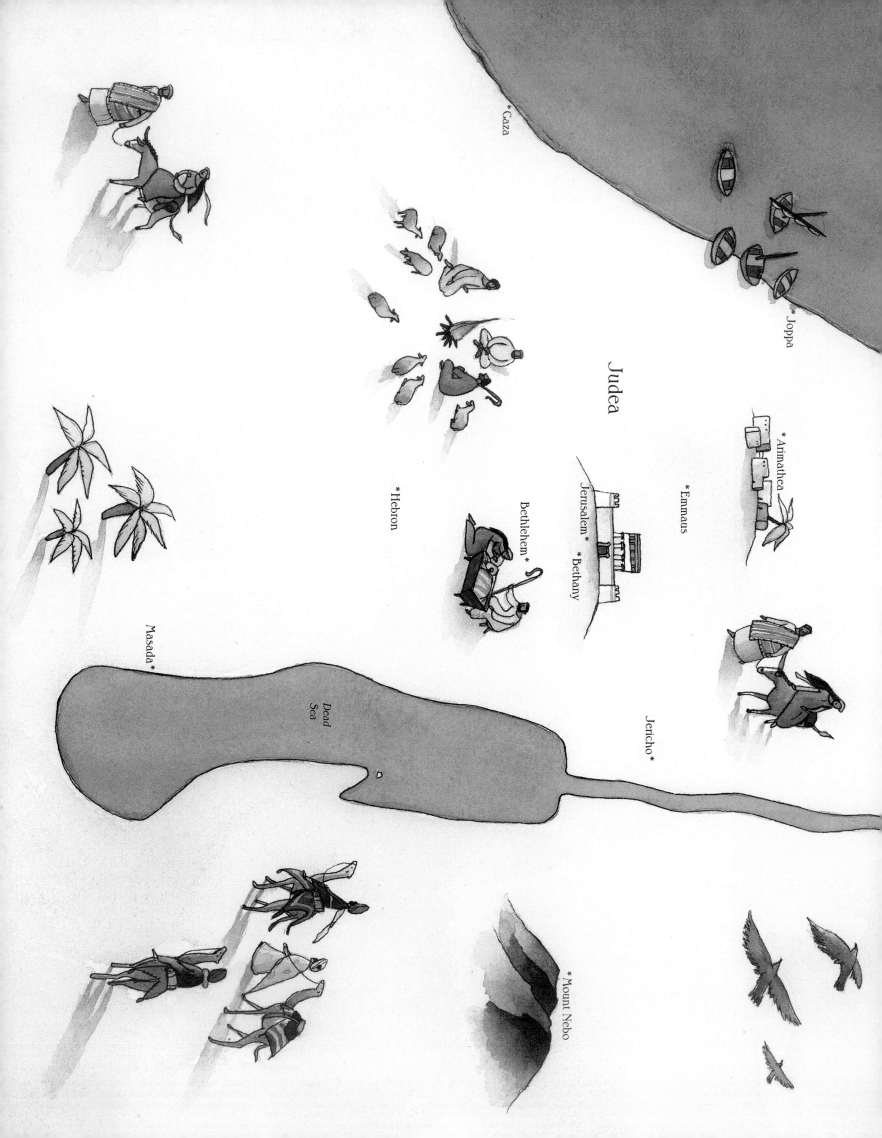

*Gaza

Joppa*

Judea

*Arimathea

*Emmaus

*Hebron

Jerusalem *
Bethlehem * * Bethany

Masada*

Dead
Sea

Jericho *

*Mount Nebo

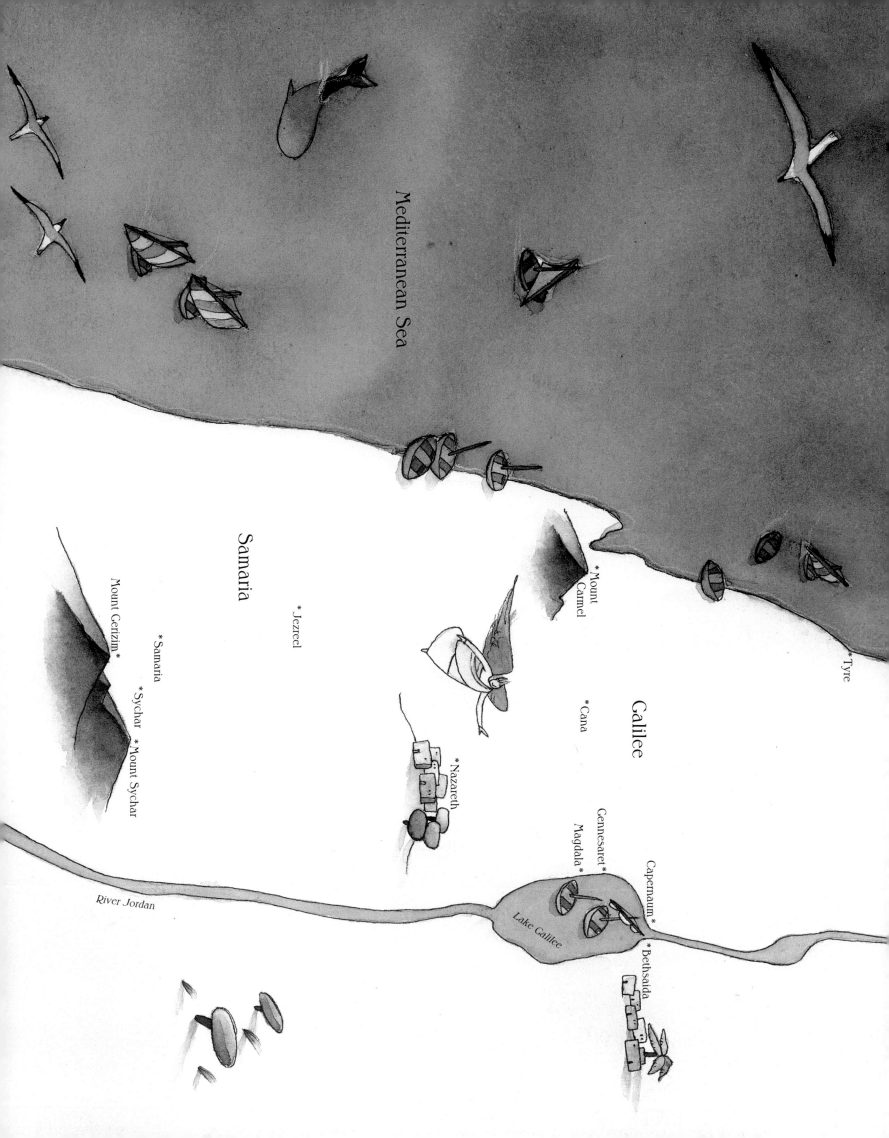

Mediterranean Sea

Samaria

Galilee

*Mount Carmel

*Tyre

*Cana

*Jezreel

Mount Gerizim *

*Samaria

*Sychar

*Mount Sychar

*Nazareth

Gennesaret *

Magdala *

Capernaum *

River Jordan

Lake Galilee

*Bethsaida

Who's who

Anna: a very old lady who saw Jesus in the Temple in Jerusalem. She knew he would save God's people.

Gabriel: the angel who told Mary that she would give birth to a son whose name would be Jesus.

Hebrews: the name of the Jewish people, also known as Israelites and Jews.

Herod the Great: the governor of Galilee and King of Judaea. He heard of the birth of Jesus from the wise men and tried to have him killed.

Israel: the name given to Jacob whose sons fathered the twelve tribes of Israel. They later settled in the Promised Land; Israel is also the name of the kingdom.

Israelites: God's special people. They went to live in

Israel, the Promised Land, and were also known as Hebrews and Jews.

Jesus: believed by Christians to be the Son of God. His life, teaching, miracles, death and resurrection are the subject of the New Testament.

Jews: God's special people. They were also known as Hebrews and Israelites.

Joseph: Mary's husband.

Mary: the mother of Jesus.

Simeon: an old man. God had promised he wouldn't die until he had seen Jesus.

Wise men: men who saw a bright star in the East and followed it to Bethlehem to find Jesus.